W9-AOY-421

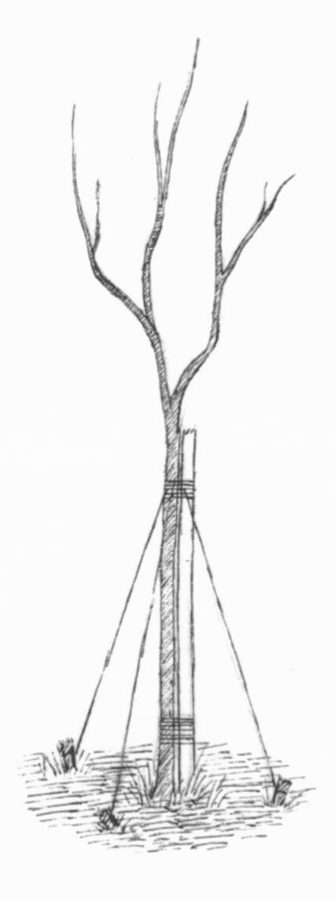

A LITTLE AT A TIME

A LITTLE AT A TIME

By David A. Adler

Illustrated by N. M. Bodecker

Random House New York

Published in the United States by Random House, Inc., New York, and simultaneously in Canada by Random House of Canada Limited, Toronto.

Library of Congress Cataloging in Publication Data
Adler, David A A little at a time.
SUMMARY: Things grow and change a little at a time, as a grandfather explains to his grandson. [1. Change–Fiction. 2. Grandparents–Fiction] I. Bodecker, N.M. II. Title.
PZ7.A2615Li [E] 75-8068. ISBN 0-394-82533-0. ISBN 0-394-92533-5 lib. bdg.

Manufactured in the United States of America 1 2 3 4 5 6 7 8 9 0

With love,

to Renée

How did that tree get to be so tall, Grandpa?
How did it get so tall?

When it started
it was just a seed.
Then it grew
and grew and grew and grew,
but it only grew
a little at a time.

And how come I'm so small?

When I was your age
I was smaller than you.
You'll grow,
not as tall as that tree,
but maybe taller than me.
You'll grow
the way I grew,
a little at a time.

How did this hole get to be so deep?
How did it get so deep?

Watch that steam shovel.
Each time the shovel drops down
and digs up some dirt,
the hole gets deeper.

But Grandpa,
the hole doesn't look any deeper.

But it is!
It's just hard to notice
when something changes
a little at a time.

Were the buildings here always this high, Grandpa?

Buildings here were much smaller
when I was your age.
But as more room was needed
small buildings were torn down,
and on the same land
higher buildings were built.
A city this big
is always changing
a little at a time.

67

Grandpa, why is this street so dirty?
How did it get like this?

Many people drop things.
Each person may drop
only a little,
but with so many people
dropping just a little,
this street became dirty
a little at a time.

And the air, Grandpa,
it's so full of smoke.
Why?

Cars, buses, trucks, chimneys—
all give off smoke.
And with so many things
giving off a little smoke,
the air became dirty
the same as the streets—
a little at a time.

NO
DU
“The

Look at all these steps, Grandpa.
Watch how fast I get to the top!

If you race to the top
you'll leave me behind,
and you'll be too tired
to see the museum.
Climb the way I climb,
a little at a time.

What are we going to see, Grandpa?

We'll see some moon rocks
and some meteorites,
and of course,
the dinosaurs.

But what about the big whales?

We'll see the whales
on another day.
A museum this big
can only be seen
a little at a time.

Wow, Grandpa!
What is this?

This is a skeleton
of a large dinosaur,
the Brontosaurus.

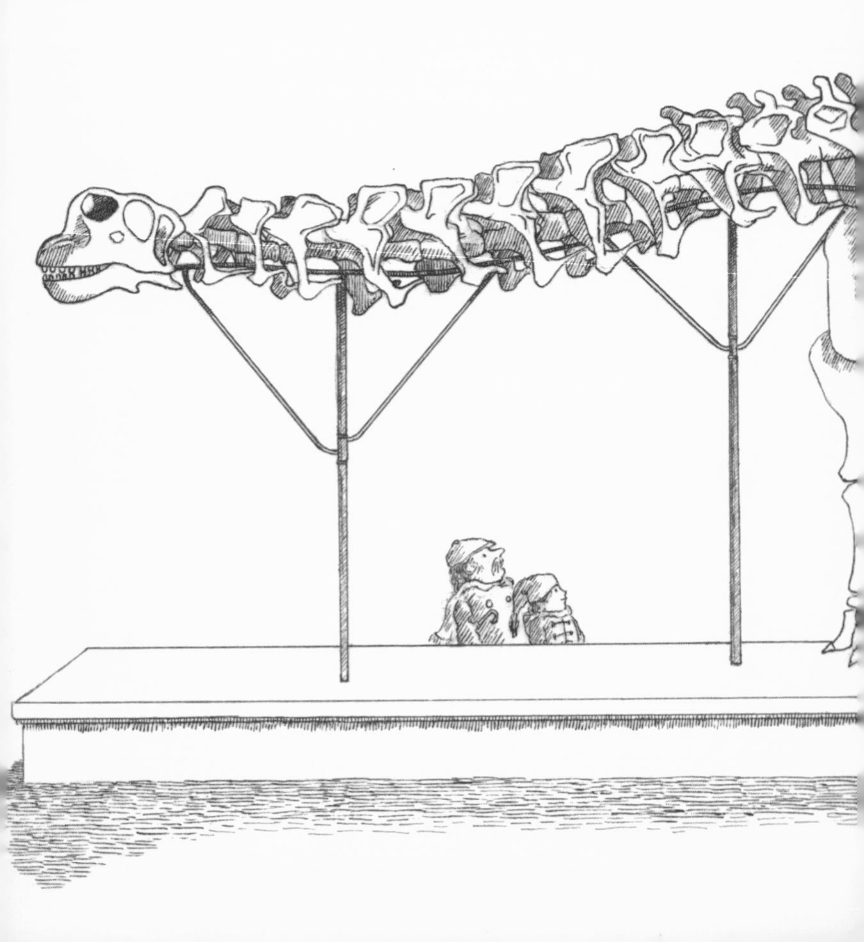

It sure is big, Grandpa.

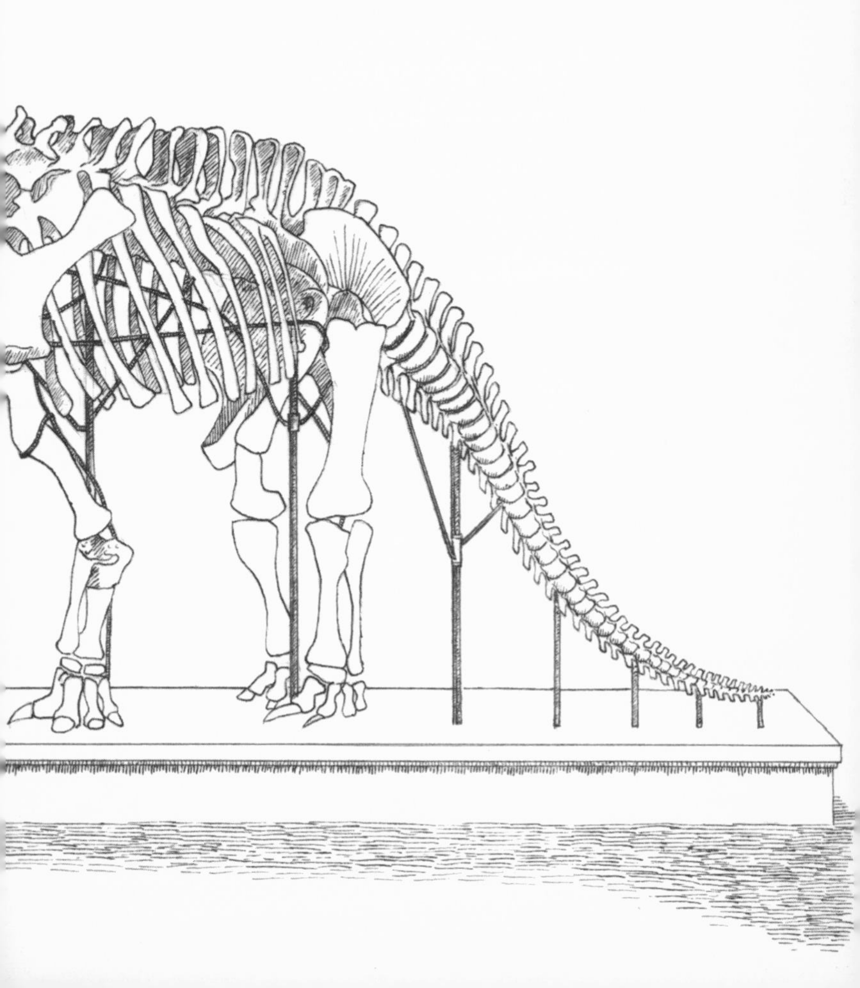

Yes,
it is big,
and it took a long time
to put it together.
Scientists dug up the bones
and cleaned them.
Then they had to learn
where each bone belonged.
It was hard work,
just like doing a puzzle.

I know how they did it, Grandpa,
a little at a time!

Come on, Grandpa;
I'm almost finished.
Why do you eat so slow?

You like ice cream
so you eat it quickly.
I like ice cream, too,
but to me it tastes better
and lasts so much longer
if I eat it
a little at a time.

It's time now
to start going home,
but don't run ahead.
Your grandpa travels
just
a little at a time.

How did you get to be so smart, Grandpa?
How did you learn so much?

I'm just like you!
I ask many questions,
and little by little
I learn a lot.
As long as I keep asking,
I'll keep learning
a little at a time.

I think it's time for my nap now.

But how did it get so late, Grandpa?

You should know the answer to that!
The day is over
very quickly it seems,
but really it went by
just like everything else–
a little at a time.